Othello

William Shakespeare

Retold by
Siddhartha Chakraborti

SCHOLASTIC
New York Toronto London Auckland
Sydney New Delhi Hong Kong

Published by Scholastic India Pvt. Ltd.
A subsidiary of Scholastic Inc., New York, 10012 (USA).
Publishers since 1920, with international operations in Canada, Australia, New Zealand, the United Kingdom, India, and Hong Kong.

First edition: May 2012
Reprint: September 2018 Nov 2019 Mar 2022 Feb 2024

ISBN-13: 978-81-8477-087-2

Printed at Ram Printograph, Delhi

The Lexile measure of this book (940L) represents the complexity of the text. This Lexile measure—along with other characteristics of the text, such as developmental level and subject matter—helps in selecting books that best match a reader's level and goals. For more information on using Lexile measures to connect readers with text, visit www.Lexile.com.

Contents

Characters

The Duke of Venice

Brabantio: *a senator*

Other senators

Gratiano: *brother to Brabantio*

Lodovico: *kinsman to Brabantio*

Othello: *a Moor, in service of the Venetian State*

Cassio: *his lieutenant*

Iago: *his ancient*

Roderigo· *a Venetian gentleman*

Montano: *Othello's predecessor in the Government of Cyprus*

A clown: *servant to Othello*

Desdemona: *daughter to Brabantio, and wife to Othello*

Emilia: *wife to Iago*

Bianca: *mistress to Cassio*

Other sailors, officers, gentlemen, messengers, musicians, heralds, attendants

1

Several centuries ago, in the city of Venice, lived a great captain who had a record of many victories. His name was Othello, and he was a Moor, but nonetheless he fought with all his might in favour of the Venetians, winning them many great victories against their enemies, the Ottoman Turks. Because of his victories, he soon became the most important and trusted of the captains who served the Duke of Venice, and rose to a position of great power and importance.

As his fame spread, he was regularly invited by important personages of the Venetian government to their houses for food and discussions. People were interested in this man, who despite being of a different race and colour, was the foremost defender of their city and its interests. Among them was an old and experienced senator named Brabantio, who had a daughter of peerless beauty—Desdemona.

Desdemona had many suitors, but her jealous father kept a strong watch on her. He ensured that she had fine education, that she was never found wanting in any way.

Although Desdemona refused all the young men who would come to court her, she was quite intrigued by the Moor.

One of Desdemona's suitors was a young man named Roderigo, who was madly in love with her. Roderigo had a friend named Iago, who was Othello's trusted flag-bearer. One night, Iago called to Roderigo to come out and meet him outside in the streets. He had fateful news—Desdemona had run off with the Moor.

Roderigo was upset and angry. 'How could this have happened?' he said. 'I hate you for not telling me about this earlier ... and all this while I thought you to be such a good friend that I even let you use my money as if it were your own!'

Iago assured his friend that he had no idea that Othello would run off with Desdemona, and swore that he hated his master Othello, and promised to help Roderigo like a true friend. He told Roderigo the reason for his hate. 'Three of Venice's most important noblemen took their hats off to him and asked him humbly to make me his lieutenant, the second-in-command. But he wants to have things his own way, so he side-stepped the issue with a lot of military talk and refused their request. "I have already chosen my lieutenant," he said. And who does he choose? A man who knows more about numbers than fighting! That man from Florence, Michael Cassio. He has a pretty wife but he cannot control her. And he has never even commanded men in battle. He has got no more practical knowledge of warfare than an old woman—unless you count what he has read in books, which any peace-lover can do. His military understanding is all theory, no practice. Yet Cassio has been chosen over me. My career is cut short by some bookkeeper, even though the general saw my fighting skills first-hand in Rhodes and Cyprus. This accountant is now lieutenant, while I end up as the Moor's flag-bearer.'

Iago bemoaned his fate, as being in military service in those days did not in any way guarantee promotion on the basis of service, but was merely based on favouritism. That is why he felt no loyalty towards Othello although he served him. But now he only served Othello to further his own ends. Having received no loyalty from the Moor, he felt there was nothing wrong in doing something for himself, while pretending to be dutiful and loyal in everyone else's presence.

Iago and Roderigo soon arrived at Desdemona's house. Iago then goaded his friend to incite Desdemona's father with the news of his daughter's elopement. They raised a big hue and cry. Brabantio himself came out to respond to the commotion. He shouted with all the authority of a senator. 'What is the reason for this horrible din?' Iago shouted back. 'Sir, you have been robbed. Your heart is going to break. You will feel like half your soul has been ripped out. At this very minute an old black ram is making love to your little white lamb. Wake up, wake up, get dressed and ring a bell, and wake all the snoring citizens. If you wait too long you will have black devils for grandchildren!'

Brabantio thought that some crazy men had disturbed his sleep, but he soon recognised Roderigo as one of the many men who were trying to woo his daughter. He thought maybe Roderigo had drunk too much and was creating a scene as a result. He admonished him, threatening to see to it that Roderigo was punished for creating a useless commotion. But Roderigo asked the senator to see for himself if Desdemona was sleeping in her room. Brabantio hurried inside, calling for light and raising an alarm in his household, fearing what he would discover inside.

Outside, Iago was in the middle of an explanation. He pointed out to Roderigo that while it was possible that the Venetian government would reprimand Othello, he was sure that they would not do away with his services, as he was needed to lead the Venetian army for the war which could break out against the Turks over Cyprus any day. So he could not be seen working openly against his master. However, a search party should be organised, Iago said, and mentioned that he would be with the Moor at the Sagittarius Inn.

Meanwhile, Brabantio returned, having discovered that his daughter was indeed missing. He ordered his servants to wake everyone and organise search groups. He even told Roderigo that it would have been better even if he had assented to him marrying his daughter. Roderigo for his part told Brabantio to get some armed men and follow him, as he knew where the Moor was. They left together gathering soldiers as they went, with Roderigo leading the way.

***

Iago, meanwhile, had gone to meet Othello. People were already opposed to the Moor, having learnt that he had eloped with a wealthy and beautiful Venetian heiress. Iago had successfully brought out of the citizens racially motivated reactions against the marriage of the dark Moor to the fair Desdemona. He now set to work again, this time to convince his master of his loyalty. In the process, he fought a man who was trying to harm Othello, stopping just short of killing him. Iago pretended to be concerned for his master, but Othello was confident that he would be defended by the Venetian government. He was undoubtedly the greatest general of Venice, and the duke himself was likely to intercede on his behalf. Secondly, he too was a prince and of noble birth, although not a fair-skinned Venetian. And finally, he would never jeopardise his own position and safety through such a bold escapade if he did not truly love Desdemona.

Soon, another group of people was seen approaching. Othello's lieutenant Cassio was at its head, on an errand from the duke himself. Cassio was worried. 'Many of the senators have already been summoned to the duke's palace.

The warships which have been out at sea defending Cyprus from the Turks, have been sending out messages. The duke wants to see you right away!'

Othello went to his room to get ready. Being a soldier, he could sense the urgency of the summons. Outside, Iago told Cassio about Othello's wedding to Desdemona.

Othello came back ready to meet the duke. Just then, Brabantio entered with his servants, some soldiers of the Venetian watch, and Roderigo.

Brabantio shouted, 'That's him! He is a thief!' Roderigo joined him, 'There! That is the Moor! Catch him!' Iago, pretending to be on Othello's side, challenged Roderigo to a duel. Othello however was calm. 'Put your swords away,' he said. 'They will rust in the dew.' He proceeded to reason with Brabantio. 'Sir, your age and status as a senator are enough to convince me to listen to you. You do not need to coerce me with swords.'

But Brabantio was not in a mood to exchange pleasantries. He accused Othello of putting a spell on his daughter, and keeping her in hiding. 'Anybody who has seen my daughter can tell you that a beautiful and happy young girl like her, who has refused to marry all the handsome young men of the city, would not run off with an ugly black man like you unless you charm her with dark magic. You are not an object of love but of fear. You have either tricked her, drugged her, or kidnapped her!' He demanded that Othello be forcibly arrested. But Othello refused to be drawn into a fight. He said, 'You have charged me with serious accusations. Please tell me how I can defend myself to your satisfaction, but I refuse to fight.'

Brabantio demanded that Othello be put in prison until the day of his trial. Othello told the senator that the duke had called on him, and as such, he would fail to fulfil his duties to the Venetian state if he obeyed Brabantio's orders. Brabantio accepted that it was better the matter were presented to the duke.

Brabantio was surprised that the duke was in a meeting even at that late hour, but he was sure the duke would be on his side. 'My cause is just,' he said. 'The duke and any of my fellow senators will take this grievance as seriously as if it were their own. If we allow offences of this sort, slaves and heathens will be our rulers!'

Soon the entire group was on its way to the duke's palace.

***

At the duke's palace, a heated discussion was going on, regarding the intelligence reports the fleet had been sending. The duke was worried about what the Turks were up to, and the reports did not inspire much confidence in him.

Soon a messenger from another ship came running inside the palace. 'I bring a message from Signor Angelo—the Turks are headed for Rhodes and not Cyprus!'

This news was greeted with scepticism. Rhodes was

much better defended than Cyprus. Then again, Cyprus was always more attractive a prize for the Turks.

Just then another messenger came panting in. 'Sir, the Turks sailed to Rhodes and have joined with another fleet! Now they have thirty ships, and are headed for Cyprus. Signor Montano begs you to send reinforcements immediately!'

Amidst the confusion, Brabantio and Othello arrived at the court. The duke, while sending out dispatches for help, welcomed Othello warmly, and was about to tell him about the crisis when he noticed Senator Brabantio. He exclaimed, 'Sir, I did not see you there! Welcome, welcome. Your knowledge and experience will be of help tonight.'

Brabantio was not interested in the defence of the republic that night; he had more pressing matters at hand. He broke down in front of the duke, saying 'My daughter! Oh my daughter!' with such force that everyone present thought she may have died. 'She is dead to me,' he continued. She has been tricked and stolen from me, enchanted by black magic spells, for she would not have made this mistake on her own!'

The duke tried his best to console Brabantio. He told him not to worry, and that whoever was at fault would be punished and that too to Brabantio's satisfaction. Brabantio then told everyone present that the person responsible for his grief was none other than Othello.

The duke asked Othello to defend himself. Othello

obliged. He declared that he was a simple soldier, and was not very good with words. While it was true that he had married Brabantio's daughter, the charges of sorcery were certainly false. Othello asked Desdemona to be brought to court. 'If she has anything to say against me, then you can not only fire me from my position as your general, but you may even sentence me to death,' he said.

While Iago and some of the attendants hurried off to fetch Desdemona, Othello explained how he had come to love her. He told them how, when as a guest at Brabantio's house, he would narrate stories of his life and the many adventures he had had, Desdemona would always listen with interest. She would feel sad when he told tales of woe, and express happiness when she learnt how he overcame his obstacles. Then one day she expressed something more, saying that if she had a friend like him, she would definitely love him.

Desdemona was asked to testify, when Othello declared, 'She loved me for the dangers I had overcome and I loved her because she felt for me. This is the sorcery I have used.'

The duke advised Brabantio to come to a judgement himself, since such a fine story would have won even his own daughter.

It was Desdemona's turn to speak, and she spoke of her husband in nothing but supportive terms. With due respect, she told her father that she had willingly accepted the Moor as her husband. Brabantio was surprised, and remained reluctant to give his blessing to the couple, and bemoaned the loss of his daughter instead.

The pressing military matters required Othello to leave for Cyprus immediately. Othello, despite being recently married, wanted to fulfil his responsibilities as a captain, and hence requested the duke to make suitable arrangements for his new wife. The duke thought she could remain with her father for the duration of the war, but Brabantio didn't agree, and neither did Othello or Desdemona. Desdemona said, 'When I married Othello it was because I wanted to live with him. Since I am a part of him now, I need to be with this soldier and share his honour and bravery. I would be miserable without him. Let me go where he is going.'

Othello also agreed, saying that he wanted Desdemona to be by his side. He assured the duke that her presence would not make him lax in his duties.

The duke reminded him of the urgency of the situation. Othello and his wife would board the ship by nine in the morning.

The night was almost over. Iago stayed back to collect the commission on Othello's behalf and joined them the next morning. As they all left to make preparations, the duke told Brabantio, 'If your son-in-law had the colour of virtue, he would be amongst the fairest of men,' and urged him to make peace with the new couple.

Roderigo and Iago were left behind, after all their scheming met with failure. Roderigo realised that he would certainly not be able to win Desdemona anymore, and expressed his wish to commit suicide. Iago urged Roderigo not to kill himself, and assured him that he was still his friend. He advised Roderigo to sell everything he had. Sooner or later Desdemona would surely get tired of the Moor, he suggested. Roderigo would be a rich person by then, and would be able to win her easily. Grief-stricken, Roderigo agreed to follow Iago's advice.

After Roderigo left, Iago smiled and thought to himself that fools like Roderigo who are so ready to part with their money could be used with ease. He remembered the widespread rumour that the Moor was having an affair even with Iago's wife, and assured himself that he would have revenge. He decided to use Cassio's good looks as a means to acquire his position as well as avenge his slight. He struck upon an idea. 'I have got it! Cassio is a smooth-talker and a seducer of women, and slowly I will impress on Othello that he is a little too close to Desdemona. Othello will soon start to believe me. I have no doubt that he will be as easily manipulated as an ass is led astray.'

2

On the island of Cyprus, a huge storm had threatened to blow even the fortifications away. During the day, there was a very strong wind, and the sea waves were the size of mountains. Braving this weather, a gentleman named Montano, along with two of his friends, went out to the shore to check if the Turkish fleet had arrived, hoping that the reinforcements from Venice would come as well.

However, it seemed as if the storm had destroyed everything. While the three friends debated whether the Turkish fleet was still out in the open sea, a fourth gentleman joined them with cries of victory. 'The war is over! One of our ships has just docked in the harbour with the news that the storm has reduced the Ottoman fleet to debris!' Montano wanted to hear more, and he soon got to know that Cassio had just sailed into the harbour, and that Othello himself was expected to arrive shortly.

Montano stopped worrying about the Turks and prayed for Othello's safety, the Moor being stuck at sea still, in such stormy weather. He said aloud, 'I hope Othello is safe. I have fought under his command and I know him to be an excellent general.'

Cassio also came up and joined the four friends, and together they looked out for Othello's ship. Soon another sail was seen, and Desdemona and Emilia, escorted by Iago, came ashore and reached the group. Iago's skill as a navigator of ships was commended, since he had brought the ship safely through the storm and the rocks, and in very little time.

Soon another sail was seen at the horizon. While the group waited for the distant ship to dock, Cassio and the others knelt in front of Desdemona and welcomed her to the island. Iago continued to pretend that he was a coarse and honest person. However, he secretly noted how Cassio continued to behave in a flirtatious manner, kissing his wife Emilia on her cheeks, while also holding Desdemona's hand. These actions were usually considered a gesture of friendship, but could easily be misconstrued as being guided by loose morals.

At that moment, trumpets announced Othello's arrival. Othello exclaimed, 'Oh my fair warrior!' and ran into the arms of his beloved wife. The couple kissed and rejoiced as he had made it safely through the storm. Othello and Desdemona left for the castle to celebrate their reunion, while Cassio was put on guard duty for the night, and Iago entrusted with bringing the luggage into the castle.

When Iago and Roderigo were left alone, Iago immediately began poisoning his friend's mind against Cassio. He pointed out the number of times Cassio had held Desdemona's hand, and how they had fondled each other's hands. Roderigo corrected him. 'It was not an advance, but a polite gesture of friendship!' But Iago had struck the right chord, so he continued, 'They were being lecherous! Such proximity is not innocent. Did you not see how close they stood, with their breaths merged into one? Roderigo, in the present situation, how long will it be before something of gravity actually transpires?'

Roderigo slowly became convinced of the impropriety of Cassio's behaviour, and agreed to pick a fight with him. Iago managed to influence him to believe that, had Othello not been in the picture, Desdemona would have fallen for Cassio.

Iago's intent was to bring Cassio down in Othello's eyes. He explained his plan to his friend. 'Cassio is angered easily, and may try to hit you. That is exactly what you need to get him to do. I can then stir up the mob in Cyprus against him. I will make the people so angry that they will only calm down once Cassio is removed from his position. To get what you want, you need to get Cassio out of the way.'

Keeping the plan in mind, Iago assigned Roderigo to do guard duty as well, as that would ensure a meeting with

Cassio. After this Iago left, musing on how to avenge the Moor for having slept with his wife Emilia. Suspicious by nature, he thought even Cassio may have been sleeping with his wife, and wished to take revenge on all promiscuous men.

***

Meanwhile, news of Othello's victory over the Turks was heard across the island, as the Moor urged everyone to celebrate by dancing, making bonfires or in whatever way they pleased. Then everyone was invited to the castle for a banquet to celebrate the marriage of Othello and Desdemona.

***

After the celebrations, Othello and Desdemona were to retire to their nuptial bed. But before they left, Othello entrusted Cassio with the responsibility of ensuring that no mishaps would take place, that the party would not dissolve into chaos, and that the guards would not get too drunk.

Iago however had wicked plans, and he provoked Cassio to drink heavily. 'Come on, Lieutenant!' he urged. 'I have here a jug of wine, and these two other gentlemen want to raise a toast to the dark General Othello with you. This is a night for celebrations!'

While Cassio was being plied with drinks, Roderigo had already drunk gallons to overcome his sorrow over losing Desdemona. Iago wanted the drinking to somehow lead to a brawl with Cassio at its centre.

Iago saw Montano amongst the drinking company and started talking to him, pointing to Cassio, describing him as a man with a drinking problem. 'He drinks like this every night before he goes to sleep,' said Iago. 'He will stay up all day and night if he does not drink himself to sleep.' Montano felt sorry for Cassio.

Despite being very drunk, Cassio remembered that he was in charge of the watch. He walked unsteadily towards the battlements, followed by an equally drunk Roderigo who was all ready to provoke Cassio to fight.

Soon cries for help were heard. Cassio, while chasing Roderigo, shouted, 'Ha! How dare you try to tell me about my duties? Come, I will beat you up!' Montano tried to intervene, but Cassio had already hit Roderigo. Roderigo ran, crying for help, and Cassio started fighting with Montano for holding him back, and injured him as well. Meanwhile, the night guard came running and raised an alarm. Othello, roused by the noise, hurried out to find out what was wrong and ordered for the commotion to end. 'How did all this happen? Have we all become as barbaric as the Turks? For heaven's sake, stop this brawling!'

Soon some semblance of order returned due to the general's presence. Othello turned to Iago and asked, 'What oing on here, gentlemen? Honest Iago, you look like have something to say. Speak up and tell me who is responsible for this.'

Iago pretended to be reluctant, but after some coaxing, he informed Othello that Cassio had started the brawl with Montano, but suggested that there might have been some reason for it. By then Desdemona had also come outside to find out what was wrong. Othello saw that his wife's sleep had been broken because of the brawling, so he decided to be harsh. 'You are no longer my officer, Cassio! And let this be an example for everyone else!' He sent off Desdemona, telling her that a soldier's day was never over, and took Montano away to personally tend to his injuries. He knew it was important to make the Cypriots feel that he was not going to be partial to his own men. He needed to ensure he had their support in the face of continuous Turkish aggression.

Cassio was left alone with Iago. He bemoaned his fate and said, 'Oh, I have lost my reputation! I have lost the immortal part of myself, and what remains is merely an animal. My reputation is gone, Iago!' Iago consoled Cassio, but in his mind he was already plotting the next step of his revenge. Cassio regretted having drunk at all and failing the trust that had been vested in him. So Iago came to his aid and offered him a possible way out of his disgrace.

'Hear my suggestion,' he said. 'Othello is completely devoted to his wife and she has a lot of influence on him. Open your heart to her and ask her to counsel you about how you can get back your lost position. She is so generous and kind and ready to help that she will do even more than what you ask for. She can help you in healing the rift between you and her husband. Your problem will be taken care of, and your relationship with Othello will be stronger than ever.'

Cassio agreed to the plan since he was in such a desperate situation. Iago was happy that all was going according to plan. Now he had to ensure that Othello would see Cassio with Desdemona, and then Iago would be able to hint at a possible involvement between the two. Iago knew he would need his wife's help, so he left to set up the next part of his revenge.

3

The next morning, Cassio went to the castle hoping to meet Othello and convey his apologies. He took a troupe of bagpipers in order to wish Othello a good morning. But very soon, the clown in Othello's service came running out complaining that the nasal tone of the pipes did not impress the general. One of the musicians tried to enquire about the nature of the problem. The clown angrily said, 'Anyone who is full of hot air is a problem! If you can play music that has no sound then you may, otherwise go and vanish into thin air!' He paid them some money, and asked them to leave since Othello was not in the mood for music.

Cassio realised that Othello did not wish to talk to him and told the clown to ask Emilia to come out and meet him. Iago's wife Emilia happened to be Desdemona's handmaiden. Cassio wanted Emilia to help him find audience with Desdemona, so that he could get her to plead his case with her husband.

At that time Iago was passing by, and he told Cassio that he would not only send his wife Emilia out, but also get the Moor preoccupied with other things so that Cassio would have a chance to talk more freely with Desdemona. Unaware of Iago's devious plan, Cassio thanked him for being the most honest man of Florence.

Emilia came out to reassure Cassio that everything would be all right. She narrated how Desdemona was strongly arguing his case with Othello, and Othello himself wished to help Cassio as he liked and respected him very much, even though he had injured a very important man in Cyprus. Emilia asked Cassio to enter the castle, and assured him that he would find audience with Desdemona.

***

Inside the castle Othello told Iago to deliver some letters for the Venetian government to the captain of the ship which had brought him to Cyprus. Meanwhile Othello would inspect the island's fortifications. He told Iago to join him there once he was done with his task, and took some other gentlemen with him to make sure their defences were in place.

***

When Othello left, Emilia arranged for Cassio a meeting with Desdemona in the garden outside the castle. Desdemona told Cassio that she would do everything in her power to help him. 'You are my husband's friend,' she said, 'and you have known him a long time. I assure you, the only reason he is keeping away from you now is to appear politically correct.'

But Cassio was not satisfied. He said, 'I am afraid these political considerations may last a long time and the general might forget about my love and service. What if I lose my job and am sent away, and someone else takes my place forever?' Desdemona assured Cassio that she would not allow that to happen, and would continue to plead his case with her husband.

Othello and Iago had by this time returned from their tour. Desdemona asked Cassio to stay while she spoke to her husband. But he left when the Moor said that he would feel even more uncomfortable if he was seen trying to make his case through Desdemona.

Cassio's meeting with Desdemona did not miss Iago's sharp eyes. He said aloud, 'Ha! I do not like this!' Othello asked Iago what he meant. The Moor noticed Cassio as he was leaving. Othello asked Iago, 'Is that not Cassio?' 'Cassio, my lord?' Iago replied. 'No, I don't think so. He wouldn't sneak away with that guilty look if he saw you coming.' In spite of himself, Othello felt jealousy and suspicion creeping into his mind.

Desdemona was blissfully unaware of these thoughts in her husband's mind. She told him that someone who was currently in disfavour with him had asked her to speak on his behalf. She revealed that it was his lieutenant Cassio, who had just left. He wanted to beg the general's forgiveness. 'Dear husband,' she said, 'if I have any influence over you at all, please forgive him. In my opinion, this man respects you a great deal, and his mistake was out of naiveté rather than wickedness. Please call him back.' But jealousy was brewing inside Othello. He dismissed the suggestion and muttered something inaudible under his breath.

But Desdemona persisted and asked for a definite date when Othello would meet with Cassio. She reminded him of the time before they were married, when she would be angry with Othello, and Cassio would always take his side. She asked her husband to help Cassio like any old friend should. Othello did not look too happy, so Desdemona scolded him. 'Do not behave as if you are doing me a favour! You make such a big scene even when I ask you to do something that will be good for you. If I ever have to ask you for something that will make you undergo hardships, I wonder how terrible your reaction will be!' Othello gave in, and consented to Desdemona's request. But he begged to be left alone for some time. Desdemona left with Emilia, while Othello stayed with his malicious friend.

Iago immediately fuelled the fire of jealousy already burning in Othello's mind. The general was too numbed by the thought that his wife had been disloyal to him to question Iago's motives. Besides, he believed Iago to be a straightforward, honest sort of person. On the one hand

Iago told Othello to be wary of such emotions as jealousy, but on the other hand he suggested, 'Keep an eye on your wife, observe how she behaves with Cassio. Do not trust blindly. I know the people of Venice; they will take your trusting nature for granted. Since you are not from around here, let me tell you that their motto is not to do no wrong, but rather to make sure that no one finds out that they are doing something wrong.'

Iago continued, 'Desdemona deceived her father to marry you. So is it not possible that she could be deceiving you now to be with someone else?' Othello admitted that while he did not think Desdemona had been unfaithful, there was always a possibility that she might be in the future. Iago egged him on by pointing out the racial difference between him and his wife. 'She must have deep-seated desires to not be with a dark Moor, but a fair Venetian. Keeping this in mind, you should not restore Cassio to the position of Lieutenant right away. Wait and see if Desdemona presses you for it, and if she does then you should consider yourself right for suspecting her of having feelings for Cassio!'

Iago now left Othello to plunge into sorrow. 'A Venetian lady would surely want fair, handsome men in the spring of youth,' he thought. Just then Desdemona came back with Emilia to find out what was taking Othello so long. Seeing him sitting alone and distressed, she pulled out her handkerchief, which Othello had gifted to her once, and said, 'You must have a headache for not sleeping too well these last few days. Let me wrap this around your head, and you will feel better soon.'

Othello refused her help, and dropping the handkerchief accidentally, went into the castle with Desdemona.

Emilia picked up the handkerchief, remembering that Iago had wanted her to steal it from Desdemona for quite some time. She had no idea why, but she gave it to him anyway. What Iago intended to do was plant the handkerchief in Cassio's apartment and have Othello discover it there. He was sure that this could be passed off for concrete evidence of his wife's infidelity.

Othello was indeed finding it difficult to feel at ease. He demanded proof from Iago and threatened him with dire consequences if he failed to prove the terrible allegation he had made against Desdemona.

Iago said that he could provide circumstantial evidence. He recalled how once he had been lying in bed next to Cassio, and how Cassio had murmured 'Sweet Desdemona! Let us be careful! Let us hide our love!' Then he had held his hand tightly, thinking Iago was Desdemona, and said, 'O sweet creature! Curse my luck that you should be with the Moor now!'

Othello in his excited state believed Iago's words. But Iago was yet to unleash the handkerchief. Feigning innocence, he asked Othello, 'Have you seen a strawberry-spotted handkerchief in your wife's hand?' 'Yes, it was my first present to her,' said Othello. 'Well, it may have been,' Iago continued, 'but today I am very sure I saw Cassio wiping his beard with that same handkerchief.' Othello said that if that was true, then not only Cassio, but even Desdemona deserved death.

Iago meanwhile pledged his allegiance to the wronged Othello, who gladly made him his new lieutenant. Iago was assigned the task of killing Cassio within three days, and Othello took on himself the task of finding a way to kill his wife, who he referred to now as 'the fair devil'.

***

Meanwhile, Desdemona went to wake Cassio up, and ran into the clown. Desdemona asked him, 'Do you know where the lieutenant is lying?' The clown, finding an opportunity to engage in wordplay, replied, 'I would not dare accuse a soldier of lying!' But he promised to go and find Cassio for her anyway.

Desdemona had meanwhile noticed that her handkerchief was missing, and mentioned that to Emilia.

Soon Othello returned and Desdemona reminded him of his promise to reinstate Cassio as his lieutenant. Othello, wearied by the thought that his wife had been adulterous, changed the subject. He pretended to have a bad cold and said to her, 'Can I have the handkerchief I had given you?' But Desdemona ignored him and continued to press Cassio's case, but Othello took this to be a further sign of her undue interest in him. He informed Desdemona that she must find the handkerchief as it was a magical one, made by an Egyptian witch. According to this witch, the woman who owned the handkerchief would have the power to make her husband like her always and be by her side forever. He told her that it once belonged to his mother, and he had saved it for his wife so that she would always be as faithful to him as his mother had been to his father.

Desdemona was taken aback by the sudden ferocity with which Othello had spoken. So she changed the subject again and asked for Cassio to be reinstated. At this Othello swore at her and left.

Emilia wondered about the inexplicable jealousies that seemed to seize men. She tried to console Desdemona, saying that it was perhaps some pressing political urgency that was making Othello behave in a disgruntled manner.

Meanwhile Iago came, dragging Cassio with him, asking him to present his case again to Desdemona. Desdemona tried her best to cheer Cassio up, and then hurried away with Emilia to try and find her handkerchief.

Meanwhile a local prostitute, Bianca, who had had her eyes on Cassio for some time, came to try and entice him. Cassio apologised to her for his continued absence, and gave her Desdemona's handkerchief to make a copy of the design since he liked it very much. He said, 'I found this in my room. I must return it to whoever has lost it.' He had no idea that it belonged to Desdemona.

Bianca wailed that Cassio was interested in another woman, but he assured her that it was not true. 'I am waiting here for the general, and I must not be seen with a woman. Please leave me now, and I will make it up to you later.' Bianca left, carrying the handkerchief with her.

4

At his castle in Cyprus, Othello was deep in conversation with Iago. Iago was slowly polluting Othello's mind with thoughts of Desdemona and Cassio being happy and intimate with each other. Othello believed him without investigating the truth himself.

Iago was not one to stop, so he brought up the handkerchief again. Othello writhed in pain and jealousy and accused Iago of polluting his mind with thoughts of his wife's infidelity that haunted him like a nightmare.

Iago suggested, 'What if Cassio has bragged about lying on your wife in bed?' Othello could bear it no more. 'I will hang him and then draw forth confessions from him!' he said, fuming with anger.

Iago watched with satisfaction as his words slowly poisoned Othello's mind. Finally he called out to him. 'My lord, do you hear me?' As luck would have it, Cassio walked in at that moment. Seeing Othello so enraged, he asked Iago, 'What is the matter?'

'My lord seems to be having some kind of fit. He had one the day before and it's attacked him again,' replied Iago. Cassio suggested Iago rub Othello's temples, but Iago pointed out that the general seemed to be recovering from his fit. 'If I interrupt him now, he might froth at the mouth and his condition may worsen. Look, he is moving. Why don't you withdraw yourself while he recovers fully? I will talk to you alone later.' In this way, he managed to get rid of Cassio.

'My lord, have you hurt yourself in the head?' Iago asked Othello. 'May I request you to face the situation like the strong man you are.' Feeling betrayed, Othello cried out, 'A man who has been cheated upon in this fashion is no longer a man. He is reduced to a monster, a beast.' He begged Iago to fetch him a confession from Cassio, so that he could legitimise his anger and jealousy.

Iago then told him of Cassio's visit when he had been in his trancelike state. 'I made an excuse on your behalf and asked him to come back later so that I can talk to him alone,' said Iago. He requested Othello to calm down and listen to their conversation without revealing his presence. 'I will make him tell me the entire story of their liaison again. I will also try to find out when they plan to meet again.' He cautioned Othello not be carried away by rage and do something foolish.

After Othello went to hide, Iago mulled over his plan. He decided to talk about Bianca, the prostitute who doted on Cassio. Cassio would not be able to control his laughter while talking about her, and that would drive Othello mad. 'Given the state he already is in,' Iago calculated, 'he will easily think Cassio's laughter and gestures are in relation to Desdemona.'

Soon Cassio arrived. Iago greeted him, 'Hello there, Lieutenant.' The use of his former title made Cassio feel worse, and he expressed his desire to get his position back. Iago carefully replied, 'If you have Desdemona speaking on your behalf to the general, you will soon have your old job back.' Then he softly added, 'If you had assigned this job to Bianca it would have been done in no time.' Cassio sighed at the mention of Bianca's name, and hearty laughter followed.

Othello heard the men laugh, but Bianca's name, almost inaudibly spoken, missed his ear. Othello's jealousy drove him into a state of uncontrolled rage. Meanwhile Iago continued to heap compliments on Cassio for his manly triumph over a woman, which made Cassio laugh all the more. Othello continued to misunderstand the situation and his anger grew.

'So, I hear you two are going to marry,' said Iago. 'Do you take me to be stupid?' replied Cassio. He spoke at length about how madly Bianca was in love with him, but he did not mention her name once. Iago gestured to Othello to come closer and hear Cassio boast of his conquests. Othello did, and thought Cassio was bragging about the charm he had worked on Desdemona. In his rage, he misinterpreted every word Cassio spoke.

While Cassio was busy bragging, Bianca arrived, waving Desdemona's handkerchief at him. 'Liar!' she shouted. 'You told me that you had found this handkerchief in your room and didn't know who it belonged to. But you cannot get away with your lies anymore! This piece of cloth surely belongs to some other lady friend of yours, who gifted it to you as a token of her love. I do not want to have anything to do with it!'

Othello gasped when he saw Desdemona's handkerchief in Bianca's hands. Bianca stomped off angrily. On Iago's insistence, Cassio ran after her.

Othello came out of hiding, his blood boiling, with only murder on his mind. Iago instigated him further. 'Did you see your wife's handkerchief?' he asked meaningfully. 'And did you hear the way he was talking about her? He casually gave away Desdemona's gift to a whore!' Othello's anger knew no bounds, but he still pined for Desdemona. But Iago sternly asked him to forget about his unfaithful wife.

Manipulated, Othello claimed that his heart had turned to stone, and he would kill his wife and punish her for betraying him. Othello was torn between his love for Desdemona and his hatred at her betrayal, unaware of the mind games that Iago was playing with him. He remembered her sweetness one moment, but the very next moment he cursed her.

Knowing Othello's weaknesses well, Iago pretended to be compassionate and reasoned with him. 'If you are so affectionate towards her, why don't you accept her in spite of her infidelity?'

Reminded of her betrayal, Othello's rage resurfaced. He roared, 'How dare she cheat on me? I will chop her into a thousand pieces!' He asked Iago to get him some poison so he would be spared the pain of arguing against her arresting beauty. 'Do not poison her, rather strangle her on the bed she has contaminated with her betrayal,' said Iago. He offered to kill Cassio himself, and encouraged Othello to do what his heart desired.

Suddenly the sound of trumpets came, announcing the arrival of Lodovico from Venice, who had come on the duke's behalf. Desdemona and Lodovico came to greet Othello along with the attendants. Lodovico conveyed the duke's message to the general. Lodovico exchanged pleasantries with Desdemona, his cousin, and asked him about Cassio's whereabouts. Desdemona apprised him of the situation, begging him to fix the rift between her husband and Cassio.

Othello was only pretending to think about the duke's message. He was actually listening to their conversation about Cassio. He could not help but express his displeasure aloud, although each time he did so, he quickly pretended to be engrossed in reading the duke's letter. Both Lodovico and Desdemona were utterly confused by his behaviour and assumed that his anger was a result of the letter's contents. 'Maybe the letter has upset him,' said Lodovico. 'I think it suggests that he go back to Venice and appoint Cassio as Governor.'

Desdemona expressed her happiness out loud, as it also meant that she would be going back to her own homeland. This proved to be the last straw, and losing his temper, Othello struck her in everyone's presence, accusing her of being a shameless infidel. Lodovico was astonished at such behaviour and promptly asked Othello to apologise. Instead, Othello hurled more abuses at his startled wife and ordered her to disappear from his sight. Shocked and hurt, Desdemona wanted to leave, but Othello called her back to insult her further. Unable to bear the unfounded insults, Desdemona ran away, leaving behind a Lodovico surprised beyond his wits.

Turning towards him, Othello said that he had read the letter and would comply with its orders. He would return to Venice and reinstate Cassio to his post. Once again Iago cleverly used this opportunity to his advantage and spoke ill of Othello and elaborated on his vices, portraying him as a regular wife-beater, astonishing Lodovico even further.

***

Othello was interrogating Emilia inside the castle. 'You have seen both Cassio and Desdemona together. How could you not have suspected anything?' Emilia was honest and fearless in spite of the mad rage she was faced with. She only feared for her husband. She said, 'Why would I suspect anything? I saw no harm in their friendship. They never appeared to be doing anything wrong. They spoke aloud, never keeping their voices low. They never even sent me out of their way on any pretext.' Emilia pleaded with Othello to believe that Desdemona was an honest woman, willing to put her own life at stake. She cursed the person who had implanted this evil thought in Othello's mind and proudly claimed, 'My mistress is the epitome of chastity. If she is accused of infidelity, the purest of wives would be reduced to mere nonentities.'

Othello asked her to fetch Desdemona, and then lost himself in his musings. He could no longer trust his wife or anybody else who spoke of her innocence. It had come to a stage when for Othello, Desdemona's every action seemed to be hiding the secret of her unfaithfulness. When Desdemona came with Emilia, Othello fondly asked her to come near him and look into his eyes. Desdemona was taken aback by this sudden show of love when her husband had struck her just a while ago.

Othello asked Emilia to leave, ordering her to keep a watch at the door. As Desdemona pleaded with him to tell her what was troubling him, Othello said, 'Why should I? What do you think you mean to me that I should share my thoughts with you?' 'I am your wife,' cried Desdemona. Othello continued, 'Go ahead and swear it on God, because you will be damned to hell for swearing a lie in his name. But I forget how good an artist you are, although even the devils might mistake you for an angel!'

Desdemona kept swearing her innocence, but every time Othello retorted with an accusation. He shouted at her, asking her to leave, but Desdemona did not miss the tears welling up in his eyes. She still laboured under the impression that it was the duke's letter that had brought about this rage in Othello. Desdemona felt crestfallen and guilty. 'Believe me, sir, I had nothing to do with the duke's order,' she said. 'If you suspect my father in this regard, know that even I have lost all my respect for him.'

But Othello could not be pacified. He could bear the marks of poverty or slavery, sickness and sores, but he could not bear being reduced to a laughing stock by his wife, who had not only rejected him but also polluted herself by engaging in sexual liaisons with her husband's lieutenant.

Sensing Othello's anger, Desdemona asked, 'I hope you know that I am completely faithful to you. Have I done something to displease you, dear husband?' In response, Othello abused her by calling her a whore. Desdemona swore on God that she was being accused wrongly. But nothing she said or did could pacify Othello, whose anger was now beyond reason. Calling Emilia into the room, he handed her some money and put her in charge of locking up and keeping a watch on Desdemona.

Emilia was troubled herself to see Othello in this mad state. Her mistress was beyond any consolation. She neither had any answers, nor could she weep out loud. She was too ashamed to discuss her marital troubles with Emilia. She merely asked Emilia to lay her wedding sheets on her bed that night and requested her to bring Iago. She wanted his opinion on what she might have done to displease her husband.

As Iago rushed forth, donning a look of concern, Desdemona broke down completely and asked him if she indeed deserved the treatment Othello had given her. When Iago feigned ignorance about the entire matter, Emilia explained the developments that had taken place. Desdemona cried, 'Do I really deserve such harshness, Iago?'

Emilia was beginning to suspect that somebody else had meddled in the matter.

'I do not think anybody could go to such depths of evilness. It is impossible,' claimed Iago. Emilia started hurling abuses at the crook who she thought was defiling her master's mind, only to be scolded by Iago to keep her voice down. Desdemona begged Iago to suggest her a way of winning back her husband's love. 'I could never do what he is accusing me of! Believe me, my friend,' she pleaded. Iago consoled her and said that Othello was weighed down by the business of the state, and was therefore being irrational.

Just then the trumpets announced dinner. Iago asked Desdemona to stop crying and have some food. He promised her that everything would be sorted out in no time.

Roderigo appeared as soon as Desdemona left with Emilia. He had started to feel suspicious that Iago had made him a false promise of helping him win Desdemona. 'You seem to be making little progress in the matter, and have provided me with no opportunities to win the woman I love. You took away those jewels from me, promising me you will use them to entice Desdemona. But nothing has happened to that effect. I feel as if I have been cheated. So I will now directly go to her and convey my feelings. If she returns my jewels, I will apologise to her and take them back, and never bother her again. If she claims ignorance about those jewels, I will take you down in a duel,' threatened Roderigo.

Fearing that Roderigo would do exactly as he had warned, Iago immediately changed his tone. He said that such show of guts on Roderigo's part had impressed him. He also insisted that he was doing everything in his power to get the two of them together. He claimed that he was almost on the verge of success, and that Roderigo's desires would be fulfilled the following night, failing which he was free to stab Iago to death.

This was enough to stop Roderigo in his tracks. Iago took this opportunity to tell him about the orders from

Venice—that Cassio was to be deputed in Othello's position in Cyprus. 'Othello will leave for Mauritania with his lovely wife Desdemona, if this comes to pass. So the only way to stop him and prolong his stay is to kill Cassio,' said Iago. He informed him of Cassio's dinner plans with Bianca, and asked Roderigo to nab him on his way. Both of them left in search of Cassio.

***

As Lodovico bid goodbye, Othello insisted on walking him out. He looked much more composed than before. Turning towards Desdemona, he said, 'You may go to our room and wait for me; I will be back shortly. Send Emilia away for the night.'

Emilia was surprised to see him suddenly so composed and gentle. But she was also a little surprised that she had been asked to go on leave. However, Desdemona did not want to displease him any further. She told Emilia, 'Give me what I should wear for the night, and do as he says. That might abate his anger.'

Emilia's suspicions were growing. She wished that her mistress had never met Othello. But Desdemona was too much in love with her husband. She admitted as much. 'I love him even when he is so harsh with me; I love even his frowns and his anger.'

Emilia put her mistress's wedding sheets on her bed just as Desdemona had requested. Desdemona sighed. 'If I die before you do,' she said, 'wrap me up in those sheets, Emilia.' Emilia gently chided her for being so silly.

Desdemona was in a pensive mood. She sat down to tell Emilia the story of her mother's maid Barbary. Barbary was in love, but her lover left her. There was an old song she knew, which reminded her of her own story. She died singing it. 'I cannot get that song out of my head tonight. All I wish to do is hang my head down in despair and sing it like poor Barbary.'

Then they conversed about various other things, but the song kept coming back to Desdemona. She started singing it:

'The poor soul sat sighing by a sycamore tree,
Sing all a green willow.
Her hand on her bosom, her head on her knee,
Sing willow, willow, willow.
The fresh streams ran by her, and murmured her moans,
Sing willow, willow, willow.
Her salt tears fell from her, and softened the stones;
Sing willow, willow, willow—
Lay by these—
Willow, willow—
Prithee, hie thee, he'll come anon—
Sing all a green willow must be my garland.
Let nobody blame him, his scorn I approve ...'

But she stopped short, realising that was not how the song went. Every brush of the wind against her door made her feel that somebody was knocking at the door, but Emilia consoled her gently. Remembering the rest of the song, Desdemona began again:

'I called my love false love but what said he then?

Sing willow, willow, willow.

If I court more women you'll couch with more men …'

It was already late, so Desdemona asked Emilia to leave as per Othello's order. For one last time she called her back and sadly asked, 'My eyes itch severely, Emilia. Is it a sign that I might soon be weeping?'

Emilia consoled her again. Desdemona asked her if there were really women who cheated on their husbands. Emilia replied in the affirmative and agreed that even she would be like them if she had the opportunity. Desdemona was horrified to hear this, and said that she would never be able to do something so terrible.

Emilia assured her mistress that if a wife did go to the extent of cheating on her husband, the fault would be her husband's, not hers. Desdemona, too much in love, refused to see any reason in Emilia's words. She bid her goodnight and prayed that she would avoid following such bad examples.

5

Iago managed to convince Roderigo of the advantages of killing Cassio. Both of them waited, hidden behind a wall on a street in Cyprus, as Iago further instigated him. 'Do not fear, Roderigo, for this will certainly improve our future. Stick your sword in him as smoothly as possible. I'll wait right next to you.' Roderigo, reluctant to do the murder, murmured encouragement to himself, 'Nothing to be worried about … I just have to kill one man. And then I will have everything I have always wished for.'

Iago on the other hand was busy reflecting on his own actions and their apparent outcome. 'Roderigo has been rubbed raw like a pimple that is ready to burst,' he said to himself, 'and now, whether he kills Cassio or Cassio kills him, either murder will work in my favour. Although it is Cassio's death that would prove more favourable for me. I hope he is the one that dies.' Hearing Cassio's footsteps, he hushed up, while Roderigo struck him with his sword.

But Cassio had armour underneath his cloak, and the

blow fell flat. In an attempt to defend himself, Cassio drew his sword and stabbed Roderigo. At this moment, Iago stabbed Cassio on the leg from behind, almost crippling him, and escaped. Hearing their cries, Othello reached the scene and saw Cassio in great pain. He felt honoured that Iago had gone to the extent of murder just to help a friend. He decided to follow his example and turned his attention to Desdemona. 'Now that your lover Cassio is dead, it's your turn to die. I have removed you from my grieving heart and will punish you for your lustful infidelity,' he said aloud. Then he left, fully prepared to kill his faultless wife.

Lodovico and Gratiano, who were nearby, heard panicked voices crying for help. But it was dark, so they thought it was probably a trap and decided to return with a bigger force. At that moment, they saw a man coming their way, with both light and weapons in his hand. It was Iago who came and asked them, 'Whose voices are those, crying out murder?'

Gratiano and Lodovico recognised Cassio's voice. Cassio of course did not know that it was Iago who had instigated Roderigo into murdering him, and then stabbed Cassio himself. As the injured man continued to cry for help, Iago pretended to be concerned and asked, 'Oh, what villains have hurt you so badly?' Cassio pointed to Roderigo, who was also lying hurt nearby, moaning in pain. Before he could open his mouth and reveal to Cassio who had really been the mastermind behind the murder, Iago stabbed him to death.

Turning back to Cassio, he made a show of concern, and

bound his wound with his own shirt. At that time, Bianca happened to be passing by. Seeing Cassio hurt so badly, she was almost moved to tears. Iago asked Cassio if he suspected anyone might have commissioned his murder. But Cassio had no idea. And soon he fainted from excessive blood loss. Bianca could no longer control her emotions and cried out Cassio's name. Iago pointed towards her in an accusatory fashion and told Gratiano and Lodovico that he believed it was Bianca's infamy that had brought about all this trouble. He turned upon Roderigo's dead body and exclaimed in surprise, 'Why, the murderer is my very own friend, Roderigo from Venice!'

Being a skilled actor, he pretended to be shocked and thoroughly puzzled by all the recent happenings. He apologised to Gratiano and Lodovico for not showing them proper respect. Then he called for a stretcher for Cassio, and at the same time consoled Bianca.

By that time Cassio had come back to his senses. Iago asked him, 'The man who tried to kill you was my friend Roderigo. How is it that he was your enemy?' The confused Cassio had no answer.

When Cassio had been carried out, Iago remarked at Bianca's pale face. Trying to put the blame on Bianca, he asked the other two gentlemen to keep a watchful eye on her, claiming, 'The guilty speak volumes, even when they say nothing.'

At that point Emilia came looking for Iago, anxious to know what had happened. Once again Iago made up a story and told her, 'Cassio was attacked here in the dark by some men, and one of them was my friend Roderigo. The others escaped, but Roderigo was left behind and died at my hands. Cassio was badly hurt and has been taken for treatment.'

He asked Emilia to find out where Cassio had been for dinner, and added that this was the fate of men who frequented whorehouses. He cast a meaningful glance towards Bianca and asked, 'Does that make you uncomfortable?'

Bianca promptly answered back, 'He did have supper at my place tonight. But that has got nothing to do with this.' Having got the confession that he was aiming for, Iago immediately asked Bianca to follow them. He asked Emilia to run to Othello and Desdemona and acquaint them with what had happened. To himself he assured that the outcome of this night would finally settle his future.

***

Othello finally returned to his bedchamber with a candle, where Desdemona was fast asleep. He had already made up his mind to kill her, but his great love for his wife made him pause. He looked at her longingly, and tried to control the great turmoil in his mind. He told himself that he had enough reasons to kill her. But once again he was awed by her beauty, and decided to kill her without leaving any scar on her flawless skin. But try as he might, he could not restrain himself any longer and stooped to kiss her in her sleep. Although overwhelmed by her beauty, his determination to punish her remained stronger.

Othello's kiss awoke Desdemona. 'Is that you, Othello?' she

said. 'Won't you come to bed, my lord?' she asked. 'Have you said your prayers tonight, Desdemona?' Othello said in reply. 'Is there still any crime that you have not asked forgiveness for? This is the time, because if I kill you before you confess your crimes, you might go to hell.' Othello's voice was ominous.

Desdemona was confused. 'I feel scared of you when you behave that way, my lord. I know I am not guilty and do not know what crime you are referring to. If I have committed any sin, it is that I have loved you too much,' she replied with a heavy heart. She was filled with terror to see Othello shaking all over, biting his lower lip as if trying to restrain himself. It still did not occur to her that he had really come to take her life.

Othello started accusing her of things she did not have the faintest idea about. 'The handkerchief I had gifted you with so much love,' he bellowed, 'you gave away to Cassio! How could you? He has also admitted that he has used you unlawfully. How did you think I would never come to know? Thank God that Iago took care of everything, including your beloved Cassio!'

Othello's rage frightened Desdemona. She tried to tell Othello the truth, but in vain. 'Bring him here. Cassio will tell you the truth,' she said.

Seeing that Othello would not relent, Desdemona pleaded with her husband to not kill her. 'Please let me live for some time more,' she cried again and again, but to no avail. Othello smothered her, for fear that if he delayed it any longer, he might lose the strength to kill her.

At this point Emilia called to him frantically, asking him to open the door. Desdemona was lying still, almost dead. Othello drew the curtains around her bed and let Emilia in. She gave him the news of the violence going on outside, of how Cassio had murdered Roderigo. Othello was crestfallen that Cassio was still alive and that his revenge had been spoiled. Suddenly Desdemona cried out, 'Oh, I have been falsely murdered, and I die an innocent woman.' Bidding farewell to Othello, she breathed her last.

Othello broke down and confessed that he had killed Desdemona. 'She had betrayed me, Emilia. She was a whore who had cheated on me with Cassio. It was your own husband, who knew of all this and had told me everything.'

Emilia was stupefied. It was hard for her to believe that Iago could have been the instigator of such violence. 'My husband, you say? My husband had told you?' Not able to restrain herself any longer, she turned towards Othello and said, 'My mistress was too fond of you, never realising what treachery was under way. Iago has lied all through, and convinced you that she had been unfaithful! You can kill me too with that sword of yours, I have no fear. But I want to tell everybody of your crime before I die.'

While Othello drew his sword, Emilia started shouting out his crime. Montano, Gratiano and Iago rushed into their chamber along with some other men. Pointing towards

Iago, Emilia cursed him and asked him to confess his crime. 'It is because of your lie that my mistress lies dead right now,' she cried. Everyone present was shocked. Emilia refused to listen to Iago anymore, who kept asking her to keep quiet and ordered her to go home. Gratiano, who was Desdemona's uncle, was greatly grieved. 'Thank God your father died out of grief. Had he been here to see you like this tonight, he would have been badly hurt,' he sighed. Othello tried without success to tell them of the reason—his belief that Desdemona and Cassio were lovers. Emilia, who knew the truth, gasped on hearing this, cursing Iago even more vehemently. Iago drew out his sword to silence Emilia. She confessed that it was Iago who had made her steal that handkerchief from Desdemona.

And finally Othello realised how he had been misled by Iago. He ran to grab him, but by then Iago had stabbed Emilia and fled. Emilia died singing Desdemona's last song.

Othello was writhing in pain and guilt. He took out a sword, hardened in ice-cold water and razor-sharp. Gratiano returned at that moment and drew back in fear that Othello might hurt him.

At this time, Lodovico and Montano entered, followed by Cassio who was being carried on a stretcher. Then came some officers with Iago under arrest. Without sparing a second thought, Othello stabbed Iago the moment he was brought forward. The others quickly took away his sword.

Slowly the truth dawned on everyone. Othello confessed

to having contrived Cassio's murder, and having killed his wife himself. He apologised sincerely to Cassio. Iago swore silence and refused to speak. Lodovico handed over two letters which they had found in Roderigo's pocket, which revealed how Iago had been instigating Roderigo to kill Cassio and falsely promising to help him win over Desdemona. Othello realised how terribly he had been manipulated. 'Oh! What a fool I am!' he cried out.

The letters also revealed how Iago had planned Cassio's demotion. Lodovico asked Othello to step down as the governor of Cyprus, after which Cassio would replace him. Othello was to be put under arrest. But it did not matter—Othello was too distraught at having killed his wife. He made an appeal to everyone to not judge him too harshly. 'Remember me as someone who did not love wisely, but loved with passion, as someone who did not easily become jealous, but fell prey to wicked suggestions.' He then took his sword, and plunged it deep into his own breast, kissing Desdemona as he died. 'I kissed you as I killed you, and now I shall die upon a last kiss from you!' were his final words.

Cassio became Governor of Cyprus, and he ensured that Iago met with a fitting punishment for his malicious deeds.

Supplementary Reading

Character Sketches

OTHELLO

Othello is a brave soldier who becomes a general in the Venetian army. He is a descendant of a noble family, and fights commendably against the Turks for the Venetians. Being a Moor, he is a dark-skinned man, and much of the anger against him emerges from the prejudices against his race.

For a large part of the play, Othello is jealous and suspicious, and betrays a mad temper. While Othello loves his wife Desdemona immensely, he is never confident that she is as faithful and loving, because he is afraid Desdemona may leave him for a European man, more handsome, younger, and with fairer skin. Although Othello's characteristics are conveniently ascribed to his race by several Venetians, we must keep in mind that Othello was misled by the supremely cunning Iago, who used these race prejudices to his advantage. While it may seem that Othello is easily misled, it must also be remembered that Iago successfully deceives not only the Moor, but also several Venetians, including Roderigo, Cassio and his prostitute-friend Bianca.

DESDEMONA

Othello's wife, and Brabantio's daughter, is the ideal noble lady—cultured, refined and beautiful. She falls in love with Othello because of the stories he tells her about his many adventures and the innumerable hardships he has endured with bravery in his life. We see more evidence of her benevolence and sympathy when she tries to help Cassio after his demotion, not knowing she is falling further and further into Iago's trap and worsening her husband's jealousy. In spite of the many accusations she is faced with, Desdemona remains an epitome of faithfulness and loyalty.

She is made of steadfast qualities, and proves that she is assertive as well, choosing to marry Othello against her father's wishes, and even though his race is suspect in the eyes of the Venetians. Desdemona is the only person in the play who does not condemn Othello based on her society's prejudices against his race.

IAGO

The ensign of Othello, Iago is a Machiavellian man whose extreme maliciousness wreaks havoc on every major character in the play. He tends to suspect people he dislikes of having illicit relations with his wife. His displeasure against Cassio stems from what he perceives as the latter's unwarranted promotion to the position of Othello's lieutenant. His anger towards Othello is also likely for the same reason—because he chose as Lieutenant someone who Iago thinks is incompetent as opposed to himself. It is also possible that he is racially motivated against Othello. However, he understands people's strengths and weaknesses well and uses them to his advantage and for the furthering of his plans. All the major characters in the play are at his mercy.

Iago's attitude towards women is extremely problematic. He sees them only as quenchers of men's sexual needs. Other than that, woman are good for nothing, just cunning creatures who use their charms to trap men.

It is Iago's actions and motivations that decide the course of events in the play, making him one of the most significant characters in *Othello*.

Questions

1

a. Who is Othello?

b. Who is Iago? Why is Iago angry with Othello?

c. Who is Roderigo? How is he used by Iago?

d. What is Brabantio's complaint to the duke?

e. How does Othello defend himself in front of the duke?

f. Why does Desdemona accompany Othello in battle?

2

a. How do the Venetians win the war against the Turks?

b. How does Iago poison Roderigo's mind against Casssio?

c. Who is Montano? Why does he fight with Cassio?

d. Why is Cassio demoted? How does he plan to win back his position?

e. Is Roderigo's role as the gullible lover believable?

3

a. Why does Othello not want to reinstate Cassio?
b. Why does Iago help Cassio in meeting Desdemona?
c. How does Iago want to make Othello jealous?
d. How does Desdemona lose her handkerchief?
e. How does Iago convince Othello of Desdemona's infidelity?

4

a. Who is Bianca? How does Iago use Cassio and Bianca to further Othello's suspicion?
b. Why does Cassio want a copy of the handkerchief?
c. Why does Othello shout at Desdemona?
d. How does Iago convince Roderigo to continue helping him?

5

a. How does Iago betray Roderigo?
b. How does Othello kill Desdemona?
c. How does Emelia die?
d. How does Othello die? What is the dying act?
e. Do you think Othello had any options other than suicide after killing Desdemona?

About Shakespeare and his Plays

WHO WAS SHAKESPEARE?

William Shakespeare (1564-1616) was an English poet and playwright. He is now widely regarded as one of the greatest writers in the English language and the greatest playwright of all time.

Shakespeare was baptised on 26 April 1564 in Stratford-Upon-Avon. His father John was a glovemaker and dealer in wool. His mother Mary was the daughter of a prosperous farmer. They had eight children.

In 1582, Shakespeare married Anne Hathaway. They had three children, Susanna, Hamnet and Judith.

Little is known about Shakespeare until 1592. At this time, records show that he was living in London and writing poetry. His early plays were also written during this period.

In 1592, Shakespeare became a founding member, actor and playwright of the Lord Chamberlain's Men, a theatre company. The most famous actor in this company was Richard Burbage, who played the roles of characters like Richard III, Othello and Lear. This company was later renamed the King's Men.

Little else is known about Shakespeare's life, though he clearly earned a lot of money for his plays. He became a substantial landowner.

He died in 1616, and was buried in Stratford.

In 1623, two actors from the King's Men had Shakespeare's plays published in what is now called the *First Folio.* This contained thirty-six plays and was sold for £1.

The period during which Shakespeare lived and wrote is now called the Elizabethan age, during the reign of Queen Elizabeth I (1533-1603), during which many great playwrights, such as Christopher Marlowe and Ben Jonson, wrote.

The works of Shakespeare that survive include thirty-eight plays, 154 sonnets and two long narrative poems. Shakespeare's plays have been translated into every major language, read, performed on stage and made into films, and continue to inspire new interpretations all around the world even today.

WHY READ SHAKESPEARE?

'Shakespeare's work is the fullest expression of the dilemmas that we as humans face ... he's capable of seeing two sides of a situation so there's always drama and there's always conflict.'—Michael Boyd, RSC Artistic Director.

Shakespeare is still read and loved because his plays contain fabulous stories and wonderful characters, and are full of marvellous poetry.

Shakespeare's plays are best watched first and then read, because in performance they take on a new magic. Today many filmmakers are making films on Shakespeare's plays. You can try watching them to get a sense of how the plays would be in performance.

PLAYS AND THE THEATRE IN SHAKESPEARE'S TIME

Performances in Elizabethan theatres were very different from when you go to see a play now. The actors and the audience always interacted. Shakespeare's company had to perform against the noise of the crowd which shouted, threw fruits and tried to join the actors on stage.

Unlike the playwrights of today, writers like Shakespeare would have to present their theatre company with their ideas. The leading actors and managers would decide whether they liked it or not, and only then would the playwright proceed. This close relationship meant that the playwrights often wrote roles with a particular actor in mind.

When a play was completed, actors would receive only their lines, and not the whole play. Thus, until rehearsals started, they would not have any idea how the parts would fit together to form a cohesive play. Rehearsals were used to sort out all the details not mentioned in the script, such as songs, exits and on-stage actions.

The Elizabethan stage was different from the proscenium

stage we see in theatres nowadays. The cheaper tickets were for the groundlings, the audience on three sides of the stage. The more expensive tickets were for patrons who sat in covered seats further back. The stage was covered in straw. The wall at the back had three entrances. Above the stage was a trapdoor for lowering performers down to the stage, and on the stage itself was another trapdoor for surprise entrances and exits.